Baby's Christmas

By Esther Wilkin
Illustrated by Eloise Wilkin

A GOLDEN BOOK • NEW YORK
Western Publishing Company, Inc., Racine, Wisconsin 53404

What did Santa leave for Baby?
Let's go in and see.

Here is Baby's Christmas tree,
With the gingerbread boys and the candy canes,
The twinkly lights and the colored balls,
Green and yellow, red and blue.
Find the Star at the top of the tree,
Shining bright for all to see.
Find baby Jesus asleep in the hay,
For He was born on Christmas day.

Santa left a music box
That plays a little tune:

Rock-a-bye, baby, on the tree top!
When the wind blows the cradle will rock,
When the bough breaks the cradle will fall.
Down will come baby, cradle and all.

He left a string of wooden beads,
Pink and blue and white.

Santa left a teddy bear,

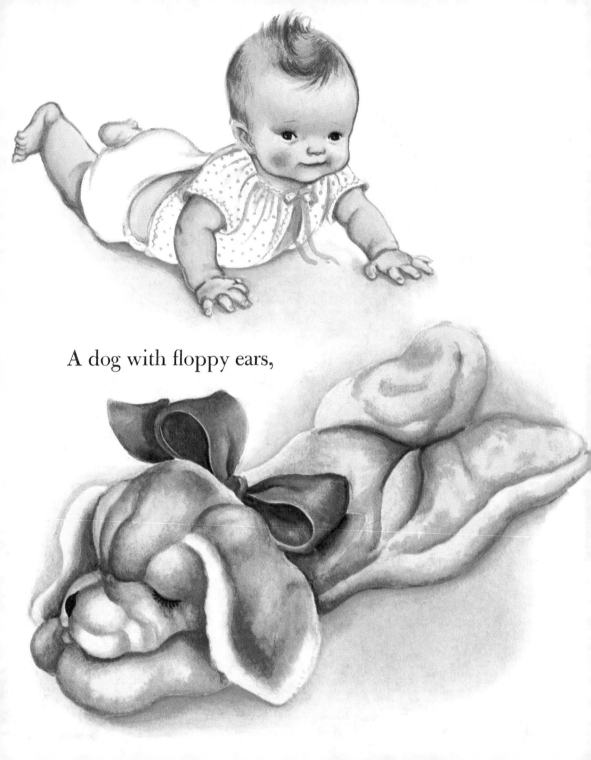

A dog with floppy ears,

A little drum to beat upon,

A kiddie car that steers.

Santa left a rubber ball
To roll along the floor,

A picture book,

a kitty cat,

And more, more, more!

A rocking horse,

A bouncy swing,

A shovel and a pail,

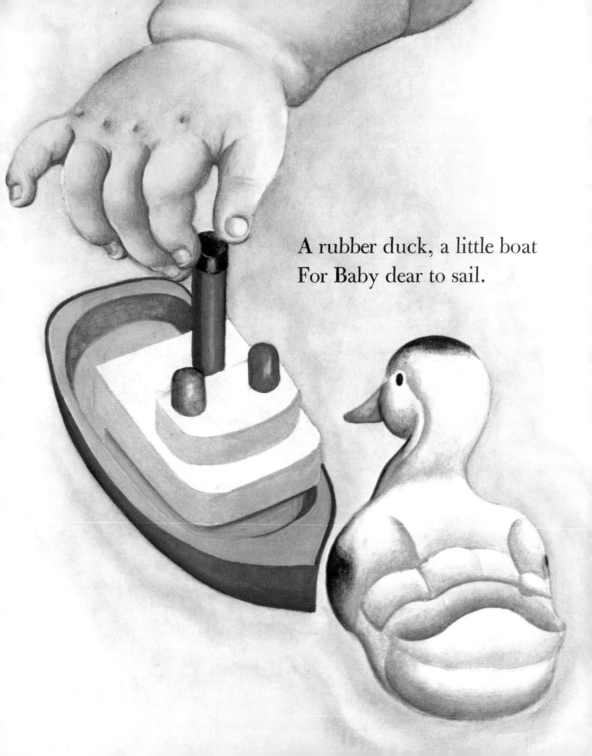

A rubber duck, a little boat
For Baby dear to sail.

Santa left some building blocks,

A milk truck,

And a train,

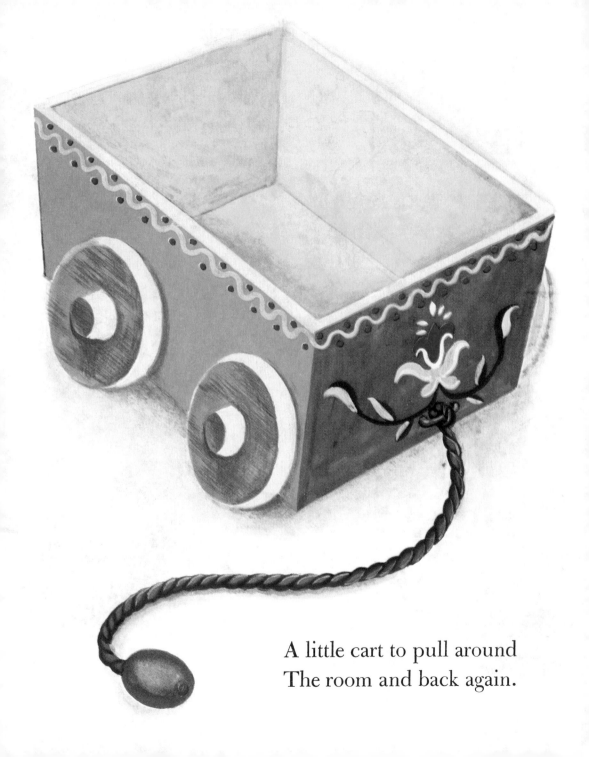

A little cart to pull around
The room and back again.

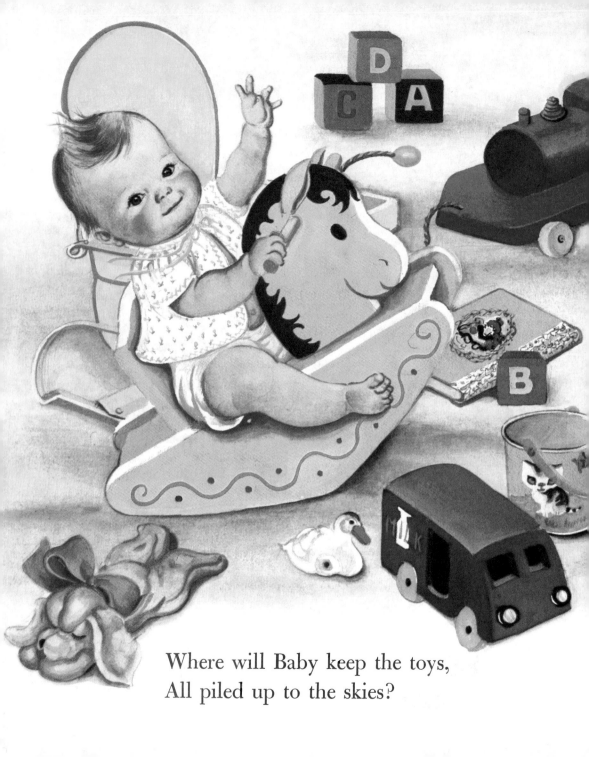

Where will Baby keep the toys,
All piled up to the skies?

Just turn the page and you will see
A great big, BIG SURPRISE!

For Santa left a toy box,
A red and yellow toy box,
So pretty and so gay!

And that's where Baby puts the toys,
At the end of every day!